MW01614294

Reconciliation Day

BIBLIOMYSTERY SERIES

#1 Ken Bruen, *The Book of Virtue*, $4.95

#2 Reed Farrel Coleman, *The Book of Ghosts*, $4.95

#3 Anne Perry, *The Scroll*, $4.95

#4 Nelson DeMille, *The Book Case*, $6.95

#5 C.J. Box, *Pronghorns of the Third Reich*, $4.95

#6 William Link, *Death Leaves a Bookmark*, $4.95

#7 Jeffery Deaver, *An Acceptable Sacrifice*, $5.95

#8 Loren D. Estleman, *Book Club*, $4.95

#9 Laura Lippman, *The Book Thing*, $4.95

#10 Andrew Taylor, *The Long Sonata of the Dead*, $4.95

#11 Peter Blauner, *The Final Testament*, $4.95

#12 John Connolly, *The Caxton Lending Library & Book Depository*, $6.95

#13 David Bell, *Rides a Stranger*, $4.95

#14 Thomas H. Cook, *What's in a Name?*, $4.95

#15 Mickey Spillane & Max Allan Collins, *It's in the Book*, $4.95

#16 Peter Lovesey, *Remaindered*, $5.95

#17 F. Paul Wilson *The Compendium of Srem*, $5.95

#18 Lyndsay Faye, *The Gospel of Sheba*, $5.95

#19 Bradford Morrow, *The Nature of My Inheritance*, $5.95

#20 R.L. Stine, *The Sequel*, $4.95

#21 Joyce Carol Oates, *Mystery, Inc.*, $6.95

#22 Thomas Perry, *The Book of the Lion*, $5.95

#23 Elizabeth George, *The Mysterious Disappearance of the Reluctant Book Fairy*, $6.95

#24 Carolyn Hart, *From the Queen*, $5.95

#25 Megan Abbott, *The Little Men*, $5.95

#26 Stephen Hunter, *Citadel*, $9.95

#27 Denise Mina, *Every Seven Years*, $5.95

#28 James Grady, *Condor in the Stacks*, $6.95

#29 Ian Rankin, *The Travelling Companion*, $6.95

#30 James W. Hall, *The Haze*, $6.95

#31 Christopher Fowler, *Reconciliation Day*, $6.95

Reconciliation Day

By

Christopher Fowler

Mysterious Bookshop

New York

Reconciliation Day
by Christopher Fowler

ISBN 978-1-61316-059-6 (Limited Edition)
ISBN 978-1-61316-088-6 (Paperback)

Reconciliation Day

Each day I expect the count to return. My work cannot be completed if he does not appear. But each day the door remains bolted, and I must return to my work again. I fear now that it will never be complete.

How well I remember the day I arrived. Never had I felt such a dread ache of melancholy as I experienced upon entering this terrible, desolate place.

The castle is less a schloss than a fortress, and dominates the mountain skyline. It is very old, thirteenth century by my reckoning, and a veritable masterpiece of unadorned ugliness. Little has been added across the years to make the interior more bearable for human habitation.

There is now glass in many of the windows and

mouldering tapestries adorn the walls, but at night the noise of their flapping reveals the castle's inadequate protection from the elements. The ramparts and walkways appear unchanged from the time of their construction. I wondered if hot oil was once poured from them onto the heads of disgruntled villagers who came to complain about their murderous taxes.

There is one entrance only, and this at the top of a steep flight of steps, faced with a pair of enormous studded doors. Water is drawn up from a central well in the courtyard by a complicated wooden contraption. Gargoyles sprout like toadstools in every exposed corner. The battlements turn back the snow-laden gales that forever sweep the Carpathian mountains, creating a chill oasis within, so that one may cross the bailey without being blasted into the sky.

But it is the character of the count himself that provides the castle with its most singular feature, a pervading sense of loss and loneliness that would penetrate the bravest heart and break it if admitted. The wind moans like a dying child, and even the weak sunlight that passes into the great hall is drained of life and hope by the stained glass through which it is filtered.

I was advised not to become too well-acquainted with my client. Those in London who have dealings with him remark that he is 'too European' for English tastes. They appreciate the nobility of his lineage, his superior manners and cultivation, but they cannot understand his motives, and I fear his lack of sociability will stand him in poor stead in London, where men prefer to discuss fluctuations of stock and the nature of horses above their own feelings. For his part, the count certainly does not encourage social intercourse. He has not even shaken my hand, and on the few occasions that we have eaten together he has left me alone at the table before ten minutes have passed. I have not seen him consume a morsel of food. It is as if he cannot bear the presence of a stranger such as myself.

I have been here for a month now. My host departed in the middle of June, complaining that the summer air was 'too thin and bright' for him. He has promised to return by the first week in September, when he will release me from my task, and I am to return home to Mina before the mountain paths become impassable for the winter.

This would be an unbearable place to spend even one night were it not for the library. The castle is either cold or hot; most of it is bitter even at noon, but the library has the grandest fireplace I have ever seen. True, it is smaller than the one in the great hall, were hams were smoked and cauldrons of soup were boiled in happier times, and which now stands as cold and lifeless as a tomb, but it carries the crest of Vlad Drakul at its mantel, and the fire is kept stoked so high by day that it never entirely dies through the night. It is here that I feel safest.

The count explained that the library had once been cared for by its own custodian and that he had died at a greatly advanced age, and then only through an unfortunate accident. He had fallen into a fast-running river and drowned.

The heat from the fireplace is bad for the books and would dry out their pages if continued through the years, but as I labour in this chamber six days out of every seven, it has proven necessary to provide a habitable temperature for me. The servant brings my meals to the great hall at seven, twelve and eight, thus I am able to keep civilised hours.

Although I came here to arrange the count's estate at the behest of my employer Peter Hawkins, it is the library that has provided me with the greatest challenge of my life, and I often work late into the night, there being little else to do inside the castle, and certainly no-one to do it with.

I travelled here with only two books in my possession; the leather-bound Bible I keep on my bedside table, and the Baedeker provided for my journey by Mina, so for me the library is an enchanted place. Never before, I'll wager, has such a collection of English, Latin and European volumes been assembled beyond London. Indeed, not even that great city can boast such esoteric tastes as those displayed by the count and his forefathers,

4

for here are books that exist in but a single copy, histories of forgotten battles, biographies of disgraced warriors, scandalous romances of distant civilisations, accounts of deeds too shameful to be recorded elsewhere, books of magic, books of mystery, books that detail the events of impossible pasts and possible futures.

Oh, this is no ordinary library.

In truth, I must confess I am surprised that he has allowed me such free access to a collection that I feel provides a very private insight into the life and tastes of its owner. Tall iron ladders, their base rungs connected to a central rail, shift along the book-clad walls. Certain shelves nearest the great vaulted ceiling have brass bars locked over them to keep their contents away from prying eyes, but the count has provided me with keys to them all. When I asked him if, for the sake of privacy, he would care to sort the books before I cast my gaze upon them (after all, he is a member of the Basarabian aristocracy, and who knows what family secrets hide there) he demurred, insisting that I should have full run of the place.

He is at times a charming man, but strange and distant in his thoughts, and altogether too much of an Easterner for me to ever fully gain his confidence, for I act as the representative of an Empire far too domesticated for his tastes and, I suspect, too diminished in his mind. Yes, diminished, for there is little doubt that he regards the

British intellect as soft and satiated, even though there is much in it that he admires. He comes from a long line of bloodletting lords who ruled with the sword-blade and despised any show of compassion, dismissing it as weakness. He is proud of his heritage and discourses upon it freely. He has not learned to be humble, even though contrition is the only civilised response to the sins of the past.

I think perhaps he regards this vast library, with its impossible mythologies and gruesome histories, as part of the bloody legacy he will have to put behind him when he moves to our country. He is, after all, the last of his line. I suspect he is allowing me to catalogue these books with a view to placing the contents up for auction. The problem, though, is that it is almost impossible for me to judge the value of such volumes. Regardless of what is contained within, the bindings themselves are frequently studded with semi-precious stones, bound in gold-leaf and green leather, and in one case what appears to be human skin. There is no precedent to them and therefore there can be no accurate evaluation.

How then am I to proceed?

A Wizzair flight from London to Romania is deceptively cheap until you realize you can't take any carry-on luggage bigger than a toiletry bag. Once I arrived I found there were compensations; a top-notch three-course meal with wine in Cluj-Napoca set me back around fifteen dollars. Hell, my morning soy-decaf-latte and Danish habit in Manhattan was almost costing me that.

I knew the country wasn't getting many tourist visits at this time of the year because everyone else in the arrivals hall was standing on the Nationals side of the passport line. They were coming home after working in England. I'd come here because of Bram Stoker, or to be more precise, because of *Dracula*.

There are people who'll tell you I'm one of the two greatest experts on that novel in the world. I prefer to think of it as a field of one. Mikaela Klove is the other and she's an antiquarian. Does that make her an expert? She's certainly grown richer on her reputation than I have, but then, it's not a big field.

Dracula's popularity is second only to that of Sherlock Holmes's adventures, but this wasn't always the case. Stoker died broke. He'd written the book in competition with a swindler called Richard Marsh, who guaranteed that he could outsell Stoker and did so that same year with a novel called *The Beetle*. Marsh annually hammered out at least three books published through sixteen different houses, and was hugely popular. *The Beetle* was his best work, but even in this Marsh couldn't resist subterfuge; his vampiric insect is actually an old man in a woman's body who can turn into a giant beetle that alters everyone it comes into contact with, smashing up the social order. Everyone in the tale shapeshifts in some way. *Dracula* was less tricksy, kind of lurid and pulpy, epistolary and fragmentary in form, and published to decidedly mixed reviews. It just couldn't compete.

The pages of the original Stoker manuscript were heavily amended by hand and signed by the author. At that point the novel was titled *The Undead,* and had several marked differences from the published version. In Stoker's manuscript, after Harker and Morris kill Dracula, the count's castle is destroyed in a kind of volcanic eruption. That's not so far-fetched; Transylvania is an earthquake region, although Stoker never went there and only saw Castle Bran, the model for the count's home, in a photograph.

The manuscript had a further significant addition, a chapter concerning Jonathan Harker's work in the castle's library, which we never encounter in the printed edition. But something odd happened—the 529-page manuscript, the only copy, vanished for nearly a century. It reappeared as if from nowhere in 1980 and was auctioned at Christie's in New York, but failed to reach its reserve price and was withdrawn. Nobody knows what happened to it after that. The story of the world's rare objects is a history of secrecy and deception.

However, there was another artifact as rare, if more apocryphal, and two people knew of its whereabouts: an old guy who ran a bookstore in Sighisoara, and Mikaela Klove, who was Lithuanian, and currently halfway through a two-year residence in Transylvania, hence my trip there.

I wouldn't call Mikaela an enemy. I guess we're friendly rivals. But she's attractive and married to a Princeton professor and she's rich enough to be able to take time off from her lecture circuit in order to work on a study of Transylvanian culture, while I'm single and close to broke and can only get a week's break before having to return to my menial day-job in New York. I'm hungrier, and I'm craftier.

You've probably already decided who the villain is in this story. The penniless chancer loses out next to the beautiful high-minded cultural expert. But you know what? Bram Stoker wasn't so high-minded. He was a pulp hack who ended up a pauper, accidentally leaving a hundred thousand critical essays by academics like Mikaela in his wake.

I picked up a hire car at Cluj-Napoca airport and headed off toward Sighisoara, to meet with the guy who had promised to show me how I could find this mythical artefact. In return I was bringing him a gift for his collection, a very rare edition of Kafka's *The Castle*. It turned out that mine was a forgery, but a very good one. By the time his waning euphoria restored his critical abilities, I'd be on my way. Of course Mikaela knew where the item was as well, but I didn't want to alert her to my interest in it. I was going to casually drop it into the conversation and see her reaction. I figured she might be able to guide me through any access restrictions.

Transylvania is in central Romania, and is bordered by spear-like mountain ranges. The car I hired was a piece of junk called a Dacia Logan, and took hills like an old man with bad lungs climbing a staircase.

I passed through villages that hadn't changed in a thousand years, accessed through avenues of trees in the tops of which sat bushes of leeching mistletoe like cranes' nests. It's tempting to use the vampiric analogy here; it looked like everyone was getting something from someone else. Tucked away from the beauty spots were the smoke-belching factories owned by rich corporations getting a great deal on slave labor, a few of them from my own homeland.

As the Dacia struggled on I was overtaken by

guys in black felt hats driving teams of carthorses, hauling logs. It looked as if the whole country ran on burning wood. The other thing I remember most about that journey was the graveyards. Every town had one built right beside its houses, as if to remind folk that they would always be surrounded by the dead.

*Regarding the library: I have devised a system that
allows me to create a table of approximate values,
and for now that must suffice.*

*First I examine the binding of the book, noting
the use of valuable ornamentation and pigments.
Then I make note of the author and the subject,
gauging their popularity and historical stature;
how many copies have been printed (if indicated)
and where; how many editions; the age of the
work, its scarcity and length; and finally content,
whether scandalous and likely to cause offence,
whether of general interest, usefulness and the like.*

*To this end I find myself making odd decisions,
putting a history of Romanian road-mapping before The Life and Times of Vlad the Terrible because the former may be of more utility in charting
this neglected territory. Thus the banal triumphs
over the lurid, the ordinary over the outrageous,
the obvious over the obscure. A fanciful mind
might imagine that I was somehow robbing the library of its power by reclassifying these tomes in
such a prosaic manner, that by quantifying them
I am reducing the spell they cast. Fancies grow
within these great walls. The castle is conducive to
them.*

*Finally I've started upon the high barred
shelves, and what I find there surprises, delights*

and occasionally revolts me. Little histories, human fables set in centuries gone by or years yet to come, that reveal how little our basest nature changes with the passing decades. These books interest me the most.

I had not intended to begin reading any of the volumes, you understand, for the simple reason that it would slow my rate of progress to a crawl, and there are still so many shelves to document. Many books require handling with the utmost care, for their condition is so delicate that their gossamer pages crumble in the heat of a hand. However, I now permit myself to read in the evenings, in order that I might put from my mind the worsening weather, my poor pining Mina and the thought that I could become a prisoner here.

The light in the library is good, there being a proliferation of candles lit for me, and the great brocaded armchair I had brought down from the bedroom is pulled as close to the fire as I dare, deep and comfortable. I am left a nightly brandy, set down before me in a crystal bowl. Outside I hear the wind loping around the battlements like a wounded wolf, and in the distant hills I hear some of those very creatures lifting their heads to the sky. The fire shifts, popping and crackling in the grate. The room is bathed in low red light. I open the book I have chosen for the night and begin to read.

Sighisoara looked shut. Its main attraction was a complete medieval village with covered wooden walkways. Around that was a town with one hipster coffee bar called the Arts Café, lots of bookshops (no English language volumes here), a couple of Russian Orthodox churches, some post-war Communist buildings finished in cheap crumbling concrete and some stunning *fin de siècle* neo-baroque houses painted in odd colors; rust red, custard yellow, lime green. I was told that during high season there were street bars and music festivals and tourists, but not in February, with wet sleet riving across the empty streets. There are a handful of shops selling tourist crap, the weirdest item being the pleading chicken, a china figurine of a bird with its wings pressed together in prayer, begging for its life. Eastern European humor; go figure.

I met up with my bookstore contact, handed the Kafka to him, watched his fingers fluttering through the pages with excitement, received an envelope in return and beat it.

As I headed into the black hills below the Carpathian Mountains the weather changed and visibility dropped. The sleet turned to great powdery flakes of snow the size of paper scraps, and soon began to settle. I spent the next six hours stuck behind filth-encrusted trucks lumbering along single-lane highways, barely getting out of third gear while the locals overtook at hair-raising speeds.

Tired of staring at tarmac and truck wheels, I pulled into a café and ate goulash and pork ribs, sluiced down with Ciuc beer. A wrinkled *babushka* who I swear looked like a crazy old gypsy woman from a Frankenstein movie came over to the table and tried to press a foot-high icon on me. The portrait of the crucified Christ had been badly printed onto plastic and glued to a piece of plywood, and wouldn't have fooled anyone from a distance of half a mile. When I explained that I didn't want to buy it, she swore at me for a couple of minutes before wandering off to sit on the other side of the café, where she ordered a pizza the size of a drain cover and sat glowering at me as she folded pieces into her mouth.

Cursed by an old gypsy woman, I thought with amusement. *All I need now is to be chased by wolves.*

I fell asleep in the Dacia. My phone awoke me nearly an hour later.

"Carter, are you here? It's Mikaela."

"I'm on my way," I said, sitting up and rubbing my eyes. The car park was a white rectangle fenced in by tall black firs. "Are we going to meet up tonight?"

"Sure, but you know I don't have the information you want."

Oh, yeah, I was going to mention that. I may have shared a little too much information with Mikaela in a drunken late-night phone call. I couldn't remember exactly what I'd told her, so I had to be careful.

"I have some leads of my own." I tried to sound as if it was no big deal. I wasn't about to explain what was in the envelope in my glove box.

"You know what you're seeking doesn't exist," she said. "The American copyright loophole was closed and the playscript in the British Library was never—"

"Don't lecture me, Mikaela. I have a pretty good idea where everything is."

"But you don't know where the edition is or if it even exists, do you?" She let the question hang in the air, probing for an answer.

"You know who I thought would be great in a new Dracula role?" I said, quickly changing the subject, "Benedict Cumberbatch. He looks like Henry Irving, don't you think?" It seemed likely that the great Shakespearian actor had been the original inspiration for Stoker's vampire, and Cumberbatch was virtually his reincarnation.

"I can see the resemblance," said Mikaela. "Whereabouts are you?"

"I'm about seventy kilometers southeast of Bran. I think. It's kind of hard to tell. There are no signs and there's a lot of snow coming down."

"It's worse up in the mountains. Call me when you get near the castle. It'll be shut by the time you get here but we can have dinner."

I agreed and hung up, reset my GPS and swung back onto the road, followed by a pack of howling feral dogs.

I have the feeling that I am not alone.

I know there are servants, four I think; a raw-looking woman who cooks and cleans, her silent husband the groom, an addle-pated under-servant born without wits who is only fit for washing and sweeping (he might be the son of the cook; there is a resemblance) and an unsmiling German butler whom I take to be the count's manservant.

But there is someone else here. I sense his presence late at night, when the fire has banked down to an amber glow and the library is at its gloomiest. I can feel him standing silently beyond the windows (an impossibility since they overlook a sheer drop of several hundred feet). When I turn to catch a glimpse of this imagined figure it is gone.

Last night the feeling came again. I had just finished cataloguing the top shelves of the library's west wall and was setting the iron ladders back in their place when I became aware of someone staring at my back. A sensation of panic seized me as the hairs stood on my neck, prickling as though charged with electricity, but I forced myself to continue with my task, finally turning in the natural course of my duty and raising my gaze to where I felt this mysterious stranger to be standing.

Of course there was nothing corporeal to see—

yet this time the feeling persisted. I made my way across the great room, passing the glowing red escarpment of the fire, until I reached the bank of mullioned windows set in the room's north side. Through the rain that was ticking against the glass I looked out on the most forsaken landscape imaginable, black pines and black rock. I could still feel him somewhere outside the windows, yet how was this possible? I am a man who prides himself on his sensitivity, and fancied that this baleful presence belonged to none other than my host. The count was not due to return for a while yet, having extended his trip to conclude certain pressing business affairs.

This presents me with a new problem, for I am told that winter settles suddenly in the mountains, and is slow to release the province from its numbing grip. Once the blizzards begin the roads will become inundated, making it impossible for me to leave the castle until the end of next spring, a full seven months away. Despite the count's relayed requests that I should write home providing departure dates, I wonder if they will materialise. If not, I would truly be a prisoner here.

With that thought weighing heavily on my mind I returned to my armchair beside the fire, fought down the urge to panic, opened a book and once more began to read.

I must have dozed, for I can only think that what I saw next was a hallucination resulting from a poorly digested piece of mutton. The count was standing in the corner of the library, still dressed in his heavy-weather oilskin. He appeared agitated and ill-at-ease, as if conducting an argument with himself on some point. At length he reached a decision and approached me, gliding across the room like a tall-ship in still seas. Flowing behind him was a rippling wave of fur, as hundreds of rats poured over the chairs and tables in a fanned brown shadow. The rodents watched me with eyes like ebony beads. They cascaded over the count's shoes and formed a great circle around my chair, as if awaiting a signal. But the signal did not come, so they fell upon one another, the strongest tearing into the soft fat bellies of the weakest, and the library carpet turned scarlet as the chamber filled with screams.

I awoke to find my shirt as wet as if it had been dropped into a lake. The book I had been reading lay on the floor at my feet, its spine split. My collar was open, and the silver crucifix I always wear at my neck was hanging on the arm of the chair, its clasp broken beyond repair. I resolved to eat earlier from that night on.

I couldn't have made the journey to the castle more atmospheric if I'd been travelling by stage-coach. Driving through the Carpathian Mountains in a snowstorm was a cool if exhausting experience. With the black firs rising all around me, I passed through endless tiny villages, usually trapped behind black-hatted woodcutters on carthorses.

The arrival at the castle itself was kind of a let-down, as the area proved more suburban than anything in the surrounding region of Brasov. At my first sight of the building I was like, *Is that it?* It was certainly a lot smaller than I'd imagined, and those photographs showing its pointed circular turrets against a background of steep cliffs must have been taken from a very narrow perspective, because it was surrounded by ugly modern houses and what appeared to be a funfair with a boating lake.

Yet when I drew closer I began to appreciate its melancholy grandeur. It was stark and un-adorned and imperious.

Mikaela was staying in a three star lodge called the Hotel Extravagance, so I checked in there too. It had a yellow plastic fascia and a life-sized model of a fat chef in an apron holding up a pig's head. We're academics, not movie stars; this was the kind of place we usually got to stay in. The receptionist was a smiling, pretty girl of about twenty who cheerfully admitted that she had been on duty for twenty-four hours. It was the standard length of a shift in these parts, she said. It made me hate kvetchy Manhattan restaurant staff even more.

"You do know it doesn't exist, right?" said Mikaela, smiling with secret knowledge. She raised a glass of *palină?* to me. Between us stood a terrifying steeple of pink sausages and pork parts, surrounded by hard-to-identify vegetables in gravy. The *palină* was a local fruit brandy invented in the Middle Ages, and tasted like it, but the local red wine proved sensational.

"Everyone said the manuscript was lost," I reminded her.

"But the missing parts aren't in the official version, which is why it never reached its reserve at the Christie's auction. It just wasn't that collectable, Carter. Stoker was never a great writer, you know that. His prose is purple and really not very interesting."

"I get that." I stabbed another sausage onto my plate. "Everybody said the same thing about the Pre-Raphaelites but look how their stock jumped. And *Dracula* will become more valued in time. You know what makes the difference? Movies. There have been nearly three hundred films made from that one book so far, almost as many as from all of Sherlock Holmes."

"But you have to face the fact that it just doesn't have the same cachet."

"All it will take is one more hit movie. How many rich, dumb collectors now think that Disney's live-action *Alice in Wonderland* characters are from the book? They're not interested in the Tenniel art but they'll pay insane amounts for studio memorabilia."

I needed to play down my own obsession. The last thing I wanted was Mikaela figuring out what I was up to. I'd read the contents of the bookseller's envelope and as I suspected, it wasn't enough to get me there without help. I'd need Mikaela but she had to make the offer unwittingly.

"It was the wrong time for the sale of the annotated manuscript," she said, spearing asparagus. "That's why it was withdrawn. You're right; its value is higher now."

"I still believe the blue edition is out there somewhere. If it's anywhere, it has to be here. I'd just like to see it once."

The blue edition—okay, what happened was this. In May 1897 Constable published the first edition bound in yellow cloth. It wasn't a success. However, an export edition was discussed. It was also to be in English but printed differently, with more widely spaced paragraphs and a blue cloth cover. Stoker approved this second limited run even though the advance was almost nothing, sent off a copy of his manuscript and waited for the paperwork to arrive.

It never came.

The theory is that the company in charge of printing it for the European market, Karnstein-Saxon, had questions about the manuscript Stoker sent them because it was different from the one they'd read in the yellow edition. It was longer—a liability for the export version—and had a different ending. There's a sole piece of correspondence from Stoker, photocopied once but now lost, admitting that he had mistakenly sent them the earlier version complete with the chapter in the library and the immolation at the end. He told them they could edit it for length if they wanted. It was obvious he just wanted the money.

But I was sure they ran off at least one copy without any cuts.

Why did I know this? Because of a little number stuck at the bottom of a page. A copy of the book was placed in a sale catalogue printed in 1905 in Brasov, Transylvania, that totaled 556 pages, not 529 pages. The book was described as having eight woodcuts (which wouldn't fully account for the higher page tally), and a blue cover. It was bought by the priest of a town called Viscria. On the receipt for the copy he had written his reason for the purchase; to form the center of a display showing how Transylvania's fame had reached the world outside. The priest hadn't died until 1979—just before the "official" manuscript failed to meet its reserve. So why would the town have gotten rid of their copy? Did they even know it was different? They'd have hung onto it, hoping it would rise in value. That's what I was counting on.

No other copy of the so-called blue edition had ever surfaced, and the early manuscript was lost. To me, that made it virtually priceless. I've always been an obsessive completist—I can't collect something without making sure I've got it all, and this was my Holy Grail. And I guess it was why I'd ended up alone. No woman was prepared to come second in my life.

"What do you know about a town called Viscria?" I asked Mikaela as casually as I could.

FROM THE JOURNAL OF JONATHAN HARKER,
SEPTEMBER 22ND, 1893

The weather has begun to worsen, and there is still no sign of the count. As the days grow shorter a forlorn darkness descends upon the castle. The skies are troubled, the clouds heavier now, ebbing to the west with their bellies full of rain. The library occupies my waking hours. It is like an origami model of Chinese paper, ever unfolding into new configurations. Just when I think I have its measure, new delights and degradations present themselves. Yesterday I started on a further set of shelves housing nautical chart-books and maps, and while reaching across the ladder to pull one stubborn tome free, I triggered the opening of a mahogany flap built in the rear of the shelf that folded down to reveal a further hundred volumes!

I cleared a space and set these books in stacks according to their co-ordinated bindings, and only once they all stood free of their secret home did I start to examine them.

I find that delicacy escapes me at this point; they were lexicons of erotica, frankly and indecently illustrated, outlining practices above, below and altogether beyond the boundaries of human nature, described in such an overt and lascivious manner that I was forced to return them to their hiding place before the servant brought me my nightly brandy, for no gentleman would wish such volumes to fall into the hands of servants.

After he had left the room I took time to examine the single edition I had left out. It was much like the others, designed more to arouse the senses than to provide practical advice concerning the physical side of matrimonial duty. The room grew hot about me as I turned the pages, and I was forced to move back from the fireplace. The drawings were shameless, representing actions one would scarcely countenance in the darkest woods, here presented in brightest light. More shocking still was the discovery that the book was English, produced in London, presumably for foreign purchasers.

While I was examining this in detail I began to sense the presence once more, and this time I became aware of a scent, a sweet perfume akin to Atar of Roses, a scented water my own dear Mina would often dab at her swan-pale neck. The perfume, filled as it was with memories of home, quite overpowered me and I grew faint, for I fancied I saw a lady—no, a woman—standing on the staircase nearest the windows.

She was tall and handsome rather than beautiful, with a knowing look, her auburn hair swept down across a dress of sheer green gossamer, with emerald jewels at her throat, and nothing at all on her feet. She stood with her left side turned to me, so that I could not help but notice the exaggerated posture of her bosom. It was as though she intended to incite my admiration. The effect was indecent, but nothing to the effect produced when she turned to face me directly, for the front panel of her dress was cut away below her waist to reveal—well, her entire personal female anatomy, the triangle of blackness shocking against her white stomach. Stupefied by such brazenness, wondering if she was perhaps ill, I found myself unable to move as she approached.

Upon reaching my chair she slid the outstretched fingers of her right hand inside my shirt, shearing off several of the buttons with her sharp nails. I was acutely aware that the naked part of her was very close to me. Then, reaching inside the high waistband of my trousers, she grasped at the very root of my reluctantly extended manhood and brought it forward, bursting through the garment's fly buttons as if they afforded no protection. When I saw that she intended to lower her lips to this heated core of my being, every fibre of my body strained to resist her brazen advances.

Here, though, my mind clouds with indistinct but disagreeable impressions. A distant cry of anger is heard, the woman retreats in fear and fury, and I awake, ashamed to discover my desire discharged and my clothing in considerable disarray, the victim of some delirious carphology.

We didn't get drunk. Mikaela's too much of a lady and after a few shots of *palină* I figured I wouldn't be much of a gentleman. So the next morning we breakfasted early and went to Castle Bran. Around its base were dozens of wooden huts selling all kinds of cool trash; Dracula fridge magnets, keyrings, woolen hats, fur waistcoats, a snow-globe containing a castle that swirled with bats when you shook it, T-shirts printed with Christopher Lee's face, the whole schmear. Mamas in shell-suits were waddling around the stands buying vampire teddy bears while feral dogs cruised around the takeout stands, hoping to catch pieces of sausage falling from buns. But I figured hey, all this stuff didn't matter. Shouldn't castles always have peasant huts around their foundations?

Mikaela gave me a little historical background. In 1920 Bran became a royal residence and the favorite home of Queen Marie. The castle was inherited by her daughter, who ran a hospital there in World War II. It was seized by the Communists, who expelled the royal family in 1948. Cut to 2005, when the Romanian government passed a special law allowing restitution claims on properties illegally expropriated. A year later the castle was given to Dominic von Habsburg, the son and heir of Princess Ileana. In 2007, the retrocession of the castle was declared illegal because it supposedly broke the Romanian law on property and succession.

This argument between royals and the government went back and forth. In 2009, the castle administration was transferred again to Archduke Dominic and his sisters. The Habsburgs opened it to the public as a private museum to help safeguard the economic base in the region. Now it was up for private sale, so who knew if it would be safeguarded or closed down for good?

It seemed like everything else around here—undervalued and underappreciated. Every town, gallery, beach and beauty spot in France and Italy has been seen to death by cruise-ship tourists. There was no international tourism here, although I'd been told that a few visitors arrived in summer. All of which made me think that the blue edition was gathering dust in a closet somewhere in Viscria. But to get there I had to humor Mikaela, partly because she spoke the language, mostly because she was a familiar face in the area. So we went around Bran and I tried to concentrate while she told me scandalous and entirely unsubstantiated stories about the castle's long-lost library.

The interior of Bran was lacking in grandeur, and none of the mismatched fixtures were original. The bookshelves were all empty. The walls had been painted white, which destroyed the atmosphere—still, it wasn't a film set, just the inspiration for a novel. Re-reading the book on my journey I still found the prose flat and earnest, but the sense of dread accumulating in the tale excited me (HG Wells is the same, not stylistically distinguished but *Kipps* and *The War of the Worlds* always get to me). There were some details I'd forgotten—Jonathan Harker realizes the castle has no staff when he spies Dracula making the beds! The blue edition was supposed to be different in that respect too. Stoker cut the staff for the yellow edition. There was also supposed to be some erotic content the English publisher wouldn't have touched; Stoker had apparently gotten himself a little over-excited and European.

In the courtyard, the castle was criss-crossed with narrow open-sided corridors, winding staircases, spires, turrets and a deep well that conjured up memories of old Hammer films. There were hardly any other visitors.

I was just thinking about how to raise the subject of the book when Mikaela said, "I can take you to Viscria if you want."

The snow has started falling. During these increasingly frequent squalls, all sights and sounds are obscured by a deadening white veil that seals us in the sky. From my bedroom window I can see that the road to the castle is already becoming obscured. If the count does not return soon, I really do not see how I shall be able to leave. I suppose I could demand that a carriage be fetched from the nearest village, but I fear that such an action would offend my host, who must surely reappear any day now.

I am worried about my beloved Mina. I have not heard from her inside a month, and yet if I am truthful there is a part of me that is glad to be imprisoned here within the castle, for the library continues to reveal paths I feel no decent God-fearing Englishman has ever explored.

I do not mean to sound so mysterious, but truly something strange weighs upon my mind. It is this; by day I follow the same routine, logging the books and entering them into the great ledgers my host provided for the purpose, but each night, after I have supped and read my customary pages beside the fire, I allow myself to fall into a light sleep and then—

—then my freedom begins as I dream or awaken to such unholy horrors and delights that I can barely bring myself to describe them.

Some nights bring swarms of bats, musty-smelling airborne rodents with leathery wings, needle teeth and blind eyes. Sometimes the ancestors of Vlad Drakul appear at the windows in bloody tableaux, frozen in the act of hacking off the heads of their enemies. Men appear skewered on tempered spikes, thrusting themselves deeper onto the razor-sharp poles in the throes of obscene pleasure. Even the count himself pays his respects, his bony alabaster features peering at me through the wintry mist as if trying to bridge the chasm between our two civilisations. And sometimes the women come.

Ah, the women.

These females are unlike any we have in England. They do not accompany themselves on the pianoforte, they do not sew demurely by the fire. Their prowess is focussed in an entirely different area. They kneel and disrobe each other before me, and caress themselves, and turn their rumps toward me in expectation. I would like to tell you that I resist, that I think of my fiancée waiting patiently at home, and recite psalms from my Bible to strengthen my will, but I do not, and so I am damned by the actions I take to slake my decadent desires.

Who are these people who come to me in nightly fever-dreams? Do I conjure them or do they draw something from me? It is as if the count knows my innermost thoughts and caters for them accord-

33

ingly. Yet I know for a fact that he has not returned to the castle, for when I look from the window I see that there are no cart-tracks on the road outside. The snow remains entirely unbroken.

Yesterday I tried the main door and found it locked. Yet there are times when I do not wish to leave this terrible place, for to do so would mean forsaking the library. Presumably it is to be packed and shipped to London, and this gives me hope, that I might travel with the volumes and protect them from division. For the strength of a library exists in the sum of its books. Only by studying it as a whole—indeed, only by reading every single edition contained within—can one hope to divine the true nature of its owner.

"Is this it?"

I tried to see through the windshield but one wiper had stopped working. It was snowing lightly as we passed another walled village that had barely been altered in a millennium. Only a couple of cars parked by a church set us in the present. Everything else looked like a medieval woodcut.

"It's at the end of this road," said Mikaela. "Everyone makes the same mistake with Viscria. The original walled village died and the descendants moved further back to the last town we passed. I thought I'd get to know them. They're helpful when you run out of gas, kind even, but in the year I've been here I haven't gotten to know a single one well. There's too much history. It's hard to comprehend what these people have been through."

"You're going to tell me they hang garlic and crucifixes out at night," I joked, then wished I hadn't, as we passed a seven foot painted Jesus in a field.

"No, the locals aren't vampires," said Mikaela with a straight face, "but they believe in Vlad Drakul. The guy cast a long shadow. That's why you still find paintings in bars and cafés that show him gorily impaling victims. It's his memory they honor, not Bram Stoker's. The book is just a useful means to an end, a way to hook tourists into coming here. It's a pity the area's solely associated with the vampire trade. There's a lot more to discover in places like Sibiu."

I'd heard about Transylvania's capital. It boasted a magnificently rococo French-style square as grand as anything you'd find in Paris or Lyon, but typically the locals didn't feel the need to brag about it, and visitors rarely got that far.

"So what happened to the library at Castle Bran?" I asked.

"What happened to anything here under the Communists?" Mikaela said with a shrug. "It disappeared along with everything and everyone else that genocidal maniac Ceauşescu came into contact with. The one thing he couldn't take from these people was their belief system."

I was thinking of the one thing I could take from them.

We passed a peculiar arrangement of low wooden benches rooted in a circle about thirty yards across, around what looked like a blackened tree with upright branches. The green paint on the benches looked new. "I thought you said that the village was dead."

"It is, but the villagers still gather here several times a year. Old customs never die."

The dirty chalk-white walls of the old village appeared around the next corner, leaning back from the road and tapering to red clay rooftops. We parked in a sloping field full of turkeys and made our way to the entrance.

An ancient woman with a face like a dried apple greeted us at the gate and took two RON from each of us by way of an entrance fee. On the inside, there were derelict houses beneath the thick circular wall, homes which once afforded the protection of the chapel.

"That's a lard tower," said Mikaela, pointing to one of the many turrets in the wall. "The villagers wrote their house numbers on their lard skins and kept careful accounts. They still live a communal life. And they love their books. The collection is in the Reconciliation Tower, such as it is."

We climbed the dusty plank staircase to the top of the chapel's central tower, past looms and farm instruments. In a single bookcase at the end of the top floor I glimpsed a number of leather-bound volumes. "Reconciliation Tower?"

"Reconciliation Day is when the residents present their annual statement of accounts, costs of births, funerals, crops and so on. It has to be signed by every elder, and there are severe penalties for disrespect and disobedience."

"You mean that's what the burned tree was back there? The elders sit in a circle on their benches and watch while debtors are chained up and set on fire?"

"You've been reading too much Stoker," Mikaela laughed.

I went to the book-cupboard and opened the glass case.

"I don't think you should do that," she said.

"I'm just having a little look is all," I told her. The volumes inside were old but of no interest. Most concerned crop planting and animal husbandry. All were printed in Romanian.

Mikaela seemed to make up her mind about something. "Look out of the window," she said. "See what the babushka is doing."

Old Apple-Face had retired to the outside wall and was sitting on a kitchen chair in the lightly falling snow, wearing just a thin shawl around her shoulders, doing nothing and apparently feeling no cold.

"Okay, come with me." We crossed the tower floor to a rough wooden chest of drawers. "They keep the more valuable items in here," said Mikaela. I studied the chest. It was fastened shut with a fat rusty lock.

"Is there any way we can get inside?"

"What? No." Mikaela shook his head. "Absolutely not. I once asked if I could open it and they told me it was not for outsiders."

Mikaela had always been timid and culturally over-respectful. I'd told her she needed to look at the bigger picture and think about how the world might share in the value of these finds.

"You want to get lost for a few minutes?" I asked her.

"No, you can't just break in, Carter. It's a federal offence to remove anything from a state building. You'll go home tomorrow and I still have to live here."

"Go downstairs. I'm not going to steal anything, I swear, I'm just going to take a look, okay? I won't touch a thing."

As soon as she had gone, I dug out my Swiss Army knife and worked on the lock. It slid open with embarrassing ease.

*Somewhere between dreams and wakefulness, I
now know there is another state. A limbo-life more
imagined than real. A land of phantoms and sen-
sations. It is a place I visit each night after darkness
falls. Sometimes it is sensuous, sometimes painful,
sometimes exhilarating, sometimes foul and de-
praved beyond redemption. It extends only to the
borders of the library, and its inhabitants, mostly
in states of disrobed arousal, are obscenely per-
fumed. These creatures insult, entice, distract, dis-
grace, shame and seduce me, clutching at my
clothes until I am drawn among them, enthralled
by their touch, degraded by my own eagerness to
participate in their rituals.*

I think I am ill.

*By day, my high stone world is silent and ra-
tional. The road to the castle is now quite impassable. It would take a team of mountaineers to scale
the sharp gradient of the rock face beneath us. The
count has failed to return, and of his impending
plans there is no word. The servants will not be
drawn on the subject. My task in the library is
nearly over. The books—all save one final shelf—
have been annotated and explored.*

*I begin to understand the strangely parasitical
nature of my host. His thirst for knowledge and his
choice of literature betray his true desires. There*

are volumes in many languages here, but of the ones I can read, first editions of Nodier's Infernalia, d'Argen's Lettres Juives *and Viatte's* Sources Occultes du Romantisme *are the most familiar. One element unites the works—they are all the product of noble decadence, inward-looking, inbred and unhealthy.*

Of course I knew the folk-tales about the count's ancestry. They are bound within the history of his family. How could one travel through this country and not hear them? In their native language they appear less fanciful, but here in the castle confabulations take on substantiality. I have read how the count's forebears slaughtered the offspring of their enemies and drank their blood for strength—who has not read these histories? Why, tales of Eastern barbarism have reached the heart of London society, although they are only spoken of after the ladies have left.

But I had not considered the more lurid legends; how the royal descendants lived on beyond death, how they needed no earthly sustenance, how their senses were so finely attuned that they could divine bad fortune in advance. I had not considered the consequence of such fables; that, should their veracity be proven, they might in the count's case suggest an inherited illness of the kind suffered by royal albinos, a dropsical disease of the blood that keeps him from the light, an anaemia that blanches his eyes and dries his veins, and causes meat to stick in his throat, and drives him from the noisy heat of humanity to the dark sanctum of the sick-chamber.

But if it is merely a medical condition, why am I beset with bestial fantasies? What power could the count possess to hold me in his thrall? I find it harder each day to recall his appearance, for the forbidden revelations of the night have all but overpowered my sense of reality. His essence is here in the library, imbued within each page of his collection. Perhaps I am not ill, but mad. I fear my senses have awoken too sharply, and my rational mind is reeling with their weight.

I have lost much of my girth in the last six weeks. I have always been thin, but the gaunt image that glares back at me in the glass must surely belong to a sick and aged relation. I have no strength by day. I live only for the nights. Beneath the welcoming winter moon my flesh fills, my spirit becomes engorged with an unwholesome strength and I am sound once more.

I really must try to get away from here.

I set the lock on one side.

Inside the drawers were a number of gaudy icons, all fake, priests' robes embroidered with red silk, brocaded white christening dresses, hand-stitched blankets and at the bottom, a few books. I removed the stack, checking out of the window.

Mikaela was stumping about in the courtyard, trying not to look suspicious.

The blue cover jumped out. It was entirely blank, with one gold word embossed on the spine. *Dracula.*

I had to take a moment. After all this time, thinking that maybe it didn't exist—

The book had never been opened—you can always tell a virgin copy by the way the pages seem reluctant to leave one another, the tiny ticking sound the spine makes as it's stretched for the first time, the reluctance of the covers to move further apart. It was unsullied, probably the first and last one, the only one.

Stupidly, I'd forgotten to bring my cotton gloves. I didn't want to release sweat-marks onto the pages, but I had to open it and check. The book's crimson edges had dried so that their coloring had turned powdery and dusted off on my fingertips, but its snow-white interior had no discoloration and the smell of the print was still strong.

The publication date matched. The ending

was brief but new to my eyes, describing the utter destruction of the castle. It seemed desultory and flatly written, as if it had been tacked on because the author had no other way of ending the story. I could see why he had subsequently removed it. Turning to the early section, easily the best part of the book in my opinion, I searched to see if there were any other additions.

Somehow I already knew what I was going to find. The chapter about Harker and the library was there, intact. I wanted to sit down and read it right then but had to content myself with riffling through the pages, just to prove that I was not hallucinating.

Without wasting another second, I removed the copy I'd had made from my rucksack and put it in the original's place. The only thing I'd failed to realize was that the real edition had painted edges. I felt sure no-one here would know or care, but I wondered if it had been printed that way, or if the priest had marked it himself. Whatever—back home the literary world would sit up and take notice when they saw what I had. My name would live on, forever linked to Stoker's *Dracula*.

Replacing the lock and closing it, I made my way back downstairs—but Mikaela had disappeared and my car had gone.

The babushka was still on her chair, basking in the lightly falling snow as if it was a summer's day. As my fingers were crimson with dye I made sure they were tucked away in my pockets.

"Have you seen my friend?" I asked, but she had no English and would only gesture in the direction of the turkey field. Mikaela was a heavy smoker. Figuring that she had gone off to find cigarettes I made my way over to where we had parked, the precious cargo in my backpack weighing me down.

FROM THE JOURNAL OF JONATHAN HARKER,
DECEMBER 18TH, 1893

*The count has finally returned, paradoxically
bringing fresh spirits into the castle.*

*For the life of me I cannot see how he arrived
here, as one section of the pathway has fallen away
into the valley. Last night he came down to dinner,
and was in most excellent health. His melancholy
mood had lifted and he was eager to converse. He
seemed physically taller, his posture more erect, his
colour higher. His travels had taken him on many
adventures, so he informed me as he poured himself a goblet of heavy claret, but now he was prop-
erly restored to his ancestral home and would be
in attendance for the conclusion of my work.*

*I had not told him I was almost done, although
I supposed he might have intuited as much from
a visit to the library. He asked that we might finish
the work together, before the next sunrise. I was
very tired—indeed, at the end of the meal I re-
quired a helping hand to lift me from my chair—
but agreed to his demand, knowing that there were
but a handful of books left for me to classify.*

*Soon we were seated in the great library, warm-
ing ourselves before the crackling fire with bowls
of brandy. It was when I studied the count's travelling clothes that I realised the truth. His boots
and oil-cloth cape lay across the back of a chair
where he has supposedly deposited them after his*

return. But the boots were new, the soles polished and unworn. I intuited that the count had not been away, and that he had passed his time in the castle here with me.

I had not imagined what I had seen and done.

We sat across from each other in the two great armchairs, cradling our brandies, and I nervously pondered my next move, for it was clear to me that the count could sense my unease.

This, I felt sure, was to be our most fateful encounter.

I waited for what felt like an age but Mikaela didn't return. I started to get cold. The turkeys were now eyeing me with suspicion. It was beginning to snow more heavily. I set down the backpack and looked at the low hills surrounding us. At first I couldn't make sense of what I saw. I thought maybe the turkeys had escaped to the nearest ridge and were now lining up to peer down at me.

Then I realized that I was looking at a line of black felt hats.

The hats rose to reveal a row of men, walking steadily toward me. It looked like a village deputation, the precursor to a lynching. They were talking quietly with one another. Each one carried a small leather-bound book.

As they reached me, I was encouraged to walk with them to the circular benches, which they filled to an exact number, leaving me without a seat. The men were so timelessly dressed that they could have existed in any era. They didn't seem to notice me.

The little books were collected and handed to the group's oldest man. As the owner of the most luxuriant mustache and beard I guessed he was the village elder. He began to read aloud, slowly and very boringly, from the gathered accounts. I wasn't their prisoner but I didn't think they'd take kindly to me leaving, especially as I had no car, so I hung around at the edge of the circle.

I only realized that my backpack was missing when I saw it being handed in to the elder, who dug around inside it and extracted every item one by one, laying each on the ground with exaggerated care, until he came to the blue edition.

Somebody lit the tree behind me.

'I could not approach you, Jonathan,' the count explained, divining my thoughts as precisely as an entomologist skewers a moth. 'You were simply too English, too Christian, too filled with pious attitudes. The reek of your pride was quite overpowering. I saw the prayer-book by your bed, the crucifix around your neck, the dowdy virgin in your locket. I knew it would be simpler to sacrifice you upon the completion of your task.' His red eyes watched mine intently. 'To suck your blood and throw your carcass to the wolves.' I stared back, not daring to flinch.

'But,' he continued with a heartfelt sigh, 'I did so need a scholar to tend my library. In London I will easily find loyal emissaries to manage my affairs, but the library needs a keeper. To be the custodian of such a rare repository of ideas requires intellect and tact. I decided instead to let you discover me, and in doing so, discover your true self. This is the purpose of the library.'

He raised a long arm, passing it over the shelves, then turned his palms to me. They were entirely covered in tiny scars.

'The library made you understand. You see, the edges of the books are marked with my blood. They just need warm hands to bring them back to life.'

I looked down at my stained and fragrant fingers, noticing for the first time how their skin had withered.

'The books are dangerous to the Christian soul, malignant in their printed ideas. Now you have read my various histories, shared my experiences, and know I am Corruption. Perhaps now you see, also, that we are not so far apart. There is but one barrier left to fall between us.'

He had risen from his chair without my noticing, and had circled behind me. His icy fingers came to rest on my neck one by one, like a spider's legs. He loosened the stiff white collar of my shirt. I heard a collar stud rattle onto the floor beside my chair.

'After tonight you will no longer need to use my library for the fulfilment of your fantasies,' he said, his steel-cold mouth descending to my throat, 'for your fantasies are to be made flesh, just as the nights will replace your days.'

I felt the first hot stab of pain as his teeth met beneath my skin. Through a haze I saw the count wipe purple lips with the back of his bony hand.

'I give you life, little Englishman,' he said, descending again. 'You will make a very loyal custodian.'

I looked from one face to the next as the villagers discussed my case. It didn't take very long for them to reach a decision. Each one in turn held out an upright fist, as if he was carrying an invisible pole.

"You can keep the book," I said, knowing that there was no point in speaking English to them but needing to say something. "If I could just read it, then I'll be on my way." I figured I could at least photograph the pages.

Two of the men walked behind me and lifted the burning tree, gripping it by the stem. When I turned to see what they were doing, I realized that it wasn't a real tree at all but some kind of engraved wooden sculpture. They discarded the upper part, scattering embers. The remaining piece, an elaborately carved hexagonal pole, was left sticking up from the ground. I was prepared to admire its workmanship until I saw that it was a sharpened stake.

Another of the men (little more than a boy, slender-necked and the only one without facial hair) walked over and kicked me onto my back with shocking ease. I landed hard on the grass, which was blackened not by fire but blood.

The men hoisted me up by my hands and feet, held me high and without any ceremony let me fall onto the stake. Crying out in unison, they stepped on my shoulders and pelvis, stamping down with as much force as they could muster.

I guess I must have screamed. I remember lifting my head and seeing this rough wood column pinning me to the earth, the bright red tip protruding from stomach, splinters sticking in my flesh like needles. In my terror I felt nothing more than a weird sensation of invasion.

The whole thing was like one of the paintings I had seen in Castle Bran; the ritual gathering of villagers, the impaling stake, the black mountains behind. All that was missing was the count himself. Past and present collapsed together. I squirmed as they fitted the top of the burning tree-sculpture back onto its base, leaving me like a pinned moth.

I was still writhing in the mud clutching my stomach when Mikaela reappeared. She studied me pityingly for a minute, then pulled me upright and slapped my rucksack against my chest.

"Get in the car," she said. "You're going home. And change your jeans first. The guy who rented this out to you will get into trouble if you leave mud everywhere." I looked down at my stomach and found no broken skin, not so much as a torn stitch on my sweater. I was unharmed. We were entirely alone. The strange tree in the circle of benches was intact. There were no footprints anywhere.

My head felt like it was breaking in half. I had to make Mikaela pull over so I could throw up on the road. In my bag was the blue edition with the white edges, the one I'd brought out with me. I looked at my hands. My fingertips were still bright scarlet, and nothing would clean off the stain.

"You really are a piece of work, Carter," she said, lighting a fresh cigarette as she drove. "You come from a country that has never been sucked dry by a parasitic invader. You were raised to think you could have anything you wanted. Well, now you've been denied something, and I hope the experience stays with you."

"You knew the book would do that?" I asked, still pressing my stomach. It had seemed so real.

"Of course. I've read the full version. You wouldn't have known not to touch it until after you had read it. The priest was smart."

"I don't understand."

"No, Carter, and you'll never be able to," said Mikaela, tapping her ash. "That's going to be your penance."

What hurt most was the realization that I could have sat down with the book and read it without touching its blood-red edges. If I had just been content to do that, I might have finally understood Stoker's true intentions for his gothic romance.

We hardly spoke again until we reached Bran,

where Mikaela had left her car. Our parting was cool. She clearly didn't expect to see me again.

I thought about what Mikaela said on the way home, but I still didn't know what she meant. Reading the original version was the one thing I would never be able to do. The story would never be fully revealed to me. After having to live with the novel's impact for over a century the Transylvanians had claimed that right for themselves. To remind me of this failure day and night I only had to look at my hands, which still bore traces of my ordeal.

I went back to New York, and it took another month before I realized that Mikaela had reconciled me to a simple truth; that the story of your life is always incomplete until it's over, and you must accept it as that.

It would be more poetically apt if I could tell you I carried my *Dracula* editions up to the roof of my apartment building in Queens and out into the sunlight, where I watched them burst into flames.

Actually I sold them to an old friend at the Mysterious Bookshop on Warren Street. I made a packet of them. The count isn't coming back. Unlike Jonathan Harker, I'm free of him at last.